Laugh-Along Lessons

5-Minute Stories

HOUGHTON MIFFLIN HARCOURT
BOSTON NEW YORK

Bonus audio books available for download at

www.hmhbooks.com/freedownloads/

Access code: laughANDlearn

CONTENTS

Hurty Feelings

Fragility was a solid piece of work.

When she walked, her world wobbled.

In the hippo game "Sink to the Bottom" she was always the first to touch mud.

Her strong jaws could
munch a field of grass
faster than any lawn
mower.

And she never cried when
she stubbed one of her toes.

Or all sixteen.

But if injured toes didn't bother Fragility, something else did.
Injured feelings.
Fragility was fragile.

When someone said, "Fragility, you look so nice today," she would wail, "You hurt my *feeeee*lings!

Nice? Do you know what else is nice? Cupcakes are nice.
So you're comparing me to a squishy cupcake."
With that she would flop on the ground and weep.

Or if someone said, "Fragility, you have such wonderful sturdy legs," she would wail, "You hurt my *feeeee*lings! Sturdy legs? Do you know what else has sturdy legs? A piano has sturdy legs.

So you think I have piano legs."
And flop she'd go, weeping.

And if someone said, "Fragility, you have such cute little ears," she would wail, "You hurt my *feeeee*lings!
Cute little ears? Do you know what else has cute little ears?
People have cute little ears.

So you think I resemble a people?"
Flop. Weep.

As time went by, the other hippos, fearing she would throw more fits, stopped speaking to Fragility, and she became a big solid piece of —

loneliness.

One afternoon all of the hippos decided to play a game of pickup soccer.

Fragility had chomped the field to perfection. She stood solidly in the goal,

making save,

after save,

after save.

All was going well until . . .

RUDY appeared.

And Rudy had an appropriate name, for Rudy was extremely rude.

"I'm going to eat your goal," he announced, "for me lunch."

The hippos gasped in horror.

"Step aside, Big Solid Thing!" Rudy bellowed at Fragility. "You're blocking me lunch. I'm hungry and I don't have all day."

Fragility was frightened, but she was a solid piece of work,
the Protector of the Goal, and thus she stood her ground.
So Rudy, who knew of Fragility's fragile feelings, decided to
dissolve her with insults.

"You," said Rudy with a smirk, "are very gray and pudgy."

"Very gray and pudgy?" wailed Fragility.
"Do you know what else is very gray and pudgy? An el . . ."
The weeps took over, and she couldn't finish her sentence.

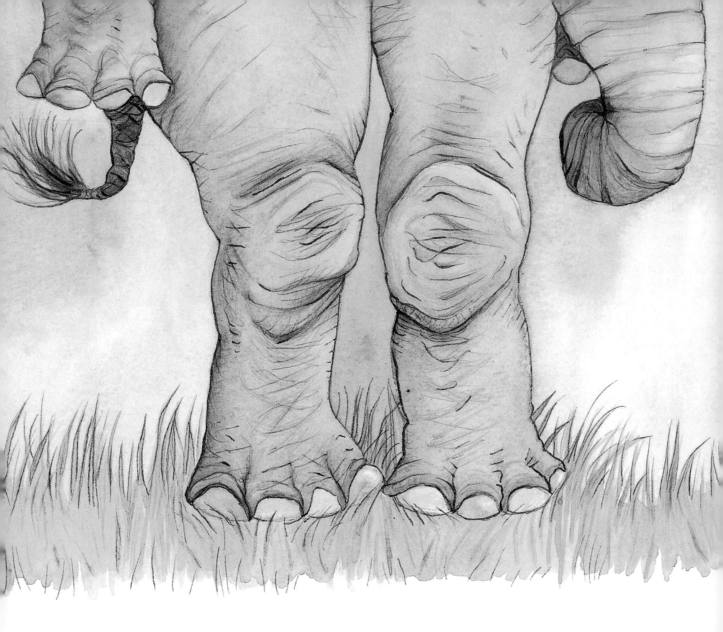

Rudy stomped his foot.
"There's no such thing as an el.
And stop weeping on me lunch.
By the way, you've got legs like tree stumps."

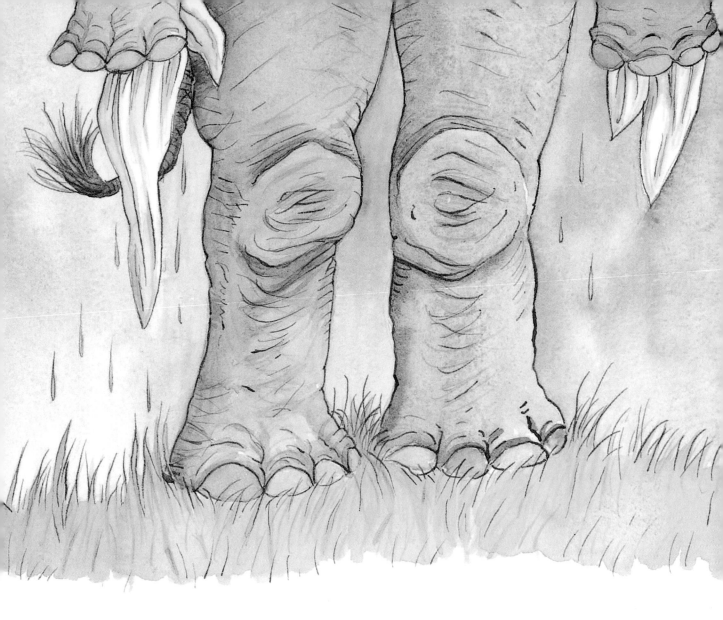

"Tree stumps?" wailed Fragility.

"Do you know what else has legs like tree stumps?

An el . . . eleph . . ."

The weeps took over, and she couldn't finish her sentence.

Rudy jumped up and down.
"I've never heard of an el eleph. And I repeat,
stop weeping on me lunch. You're making it soggy.
Have you noticed your ears are just plain weird?"

"I'm weird-eared?" wailed Fragility.
"Do you know what else has weird ears?
An el . . . eleph . . . elephant!"
Weeps and all, she finished her sentence.

"Elephant?" wondered Rudy.

"Seriously? Elephants have weird ears?"

He trotted over to the water tub and gazed at his reflection.

And his big, floppy, weird ears.

And his tree-stump legs.

And his very gray pudgy body.

Then he trotted back, flopped in front of the goal, and wailed, "You hurt me *feeeee*lings!"

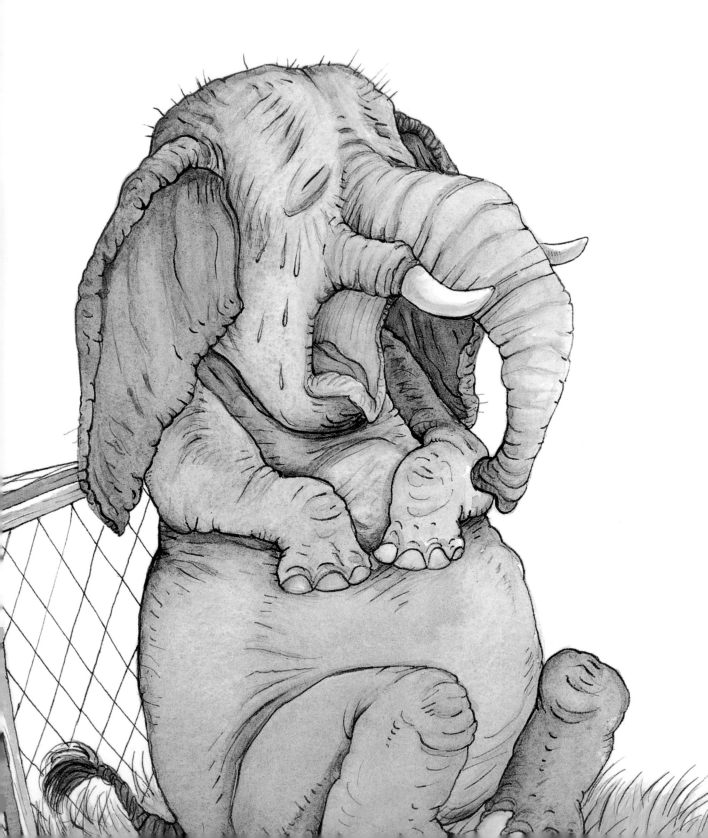

Seeing the big bully in such a state,
Fragility couldn't help but feel sorry for him.
She brought wet washcloths to soothe his red eyes,
and tissues so he could blow his trunk.

Then she cradled his head and cooed,
"There, there. I know just how you feel."

In time Rudy calmed down.
And he did not eat the hippos' goal.
He said he'd be back soon to cheer them in their game.
"But first I'm off for me lunch. A nice salad."

As he lumbered away, Rudy called, "Fragility, you're a solid piece of work."
"Solid piece of work?" she cried. "Do you know what else —"
And then she stopped short, smiled sweetly, and said,
"Why, thank you."

It Wasn't My Fault

Things did not always go well for Murdley Gurdson.

He couldn't control the toothpaste.
He fell into wastebaskets.

And he dropped only valuable vases.
Whatever happened, it was usually his fault.

One day he went for a walk
in his one too big new shoe.
He had stepped out of the other one.
He couldn't remember where.

Before long someone laid an egg on
Murdley Gurdson's head.

He looked at a nearby bird.
"Did you lay an egg on my head?" he asked.

"I did," confessed the bird, "but it wasn't my fault.
A horrible aardvark screamed and scared me."

So Murdley Gurdson and the bird
went to see the aardvark.

"Did you scream and scare the bird into laying
an egg on Murdley Gurdson's head?" they asked.
"I did," confessed the aardvark.
"But it wasn't my fault."

"A nasty pygmy hippo stepped on my tail and a scream just popped out."

Together they went to find the pygmy hippo.
"Did you step on the aardvark's tail, making him
scream and scare the bird into laying an egg
on Murdley Gurdson's head?" they asked.

"I did," confessed the pygmy hippo.
"But it wasn't my fault.
I did it by accident when I was getting
out of the way of a hopping shoe with long ears."
"A WHAT?" they all asked.

Just then along came a hopping shoe
with long ears.

With a pull and a tug, they soon found that the ears were attached to a rabbit.

"It wasn't my fault," the rabbit explained.

"I was hopping along when I landed in that shoe and became stuck."

The shoe looked very much like the new too big shoe Murdley had stepped out of some time ago.

In fact, it was.

Murdley thought:

"The rabbit became stuck in my shoe and frightened the pygmy hippo, who stepped on the aardvark's tail. The aardvark screamed and scared the bird into laying an egg on my head."

"Then I suppose it was my fault," Murdley Gurdson said very sadly.
Two tears splashed on his new too big shoes.

"There, there," said the pygmy hippo, the rabbit, the bird, and the aardvark, "don't cry."

"It was my fault," said the bird.

"It was my fault," said the aardvark.

"It was my fault," said the pygmy hippo.

"I think it was the shoe," said the rabbit.

"Let's go back to your house and do something about that egg."

They all went into the kitchen.
The aardvark turned Murdley Gurdson upside
down and the egg plopped into a pan.
The rabbit ground the pepper.
The pygmy hippo added a pinch of salt.
The bird ran around and around in the pan,
doing a very fine job of scrambling.

Murdley Gurdson enjoyed every bite of his scrambled egg.

Murdley thanked his friends.
He went to the door to let them out
and . . .

. . . it wasn't his fault!

Listen, Buddy

To Lenesa—Thanks for listening.
—H.L.

Buddy's father had a beautiful big nose.
He was a great sniffer.

Buddy's mother had beautiful big teeth.
She was a great chomper.

Buddy had beautiful big ears.

It didn't matter.

When Buddy's parents sent him to the vegetable stand to get
a basket of squash, he came home with a basket of wash.

When they asked him to buy fifteen tomatoes, he came home with fifty potatoes.

Buddy's father said, "Listen, Buddy,
will you please bring me a pen?"
"Who?" asked Buddy.
"You," said his father.
"Will you please bring me a pen?"
"A what?" asked Buddy.

"A pen," said his father.
"Will you please bring me a pen?"
"Sure," said Buddy.
Buddy's father said, "Listen, Buddy!"

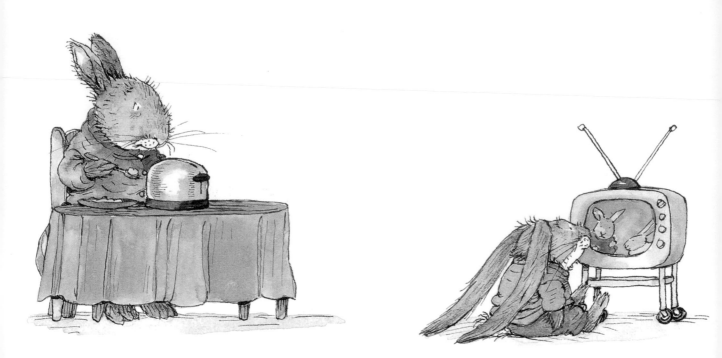

Buddy's mother said, "Listen, Buddy, will you please
get me a slice of bread?"
"Who?" asked Buddy.
"You," said his mother. "Will you please get me a slice of bread?"
"A what of what?" asked Buddy.

"A slice of bread," said his mother.

"Will you please bring me a slice of bread?"

"Sure," said Buddy.

Buddy's mother said, "Listen, Buddy!"

Somehow Buddy's mind was always wandering too far
away from those beautiful ears.
His parents tried yelling. "LISTEN, BUDDY!"

They tried whispering.
"Listen, Buddy."
Nothing worked.

One day Buddy got permission to go for a long hop.
He had never before been allowed to go beyond
the vegetable stand.

"Listen, Buddy," his parents warned him. "Just remember
that at the end of the road, there are two paths. The path
to the left will lead you around the pond and back home.
But the path to the right will lead you to the cave of the
Scruffy Varmint. And that Scruffy Varmint has a nasty
temper, so be sure to take the path to the left."

"Right?" asked Buddy.

"Left," said his parents.

"Right!" said Buddy. And with a salute of his paw he
hopped away.

Feeling very grown up, Buddy hopped along, past the
vegetable stand and on to the end of the road.
"Now let's see," he pondered. "Was I supposed to go left or right?
Or right?
Or left?"

He thought as hard as he could.
"The last thing I said was 'Right!' so that must be . . . right."
Right he went.

Twenty-five hops later, Buddy discovered that right
was wrong. There in front of his cave was the Scruffy
Varmint, doing scruffy things that varmints do, like
snarling, mussing his hair, rubbing dirt on his knees,
and scratching a whole lot of itches. At his feet was a
large soup pot.

"What are you going to do with that soup pot?"
asked Buddy.

"What does one usually do with a soup pot — bake
pie?" replied the Scruffy Varmint, not too kindly.
"I'm going to make some soup."

"Some what?" asked Buddy.

"Soup," snarled the Scruffy Varmint.

83

Buddy had forgotten his parents' warning about the
Scruffy Varmint. He asked eagerly, "May I help?"
The Scruffy Varmint was not fond of having company,
but with help he'd have his soup sooner, so he said,
"Alllll right, Bunnyrabbit, come help me gather firewood."
"Who, what?" asked Buddy.
"You. Firewood."
Buddy eagerly hopped ahead of the Scruffy Varmint.
Very gently he gathered a large prickly bundle,
which he held out proudly.

Roughly the Varmint grabbed the bundle.
"I said firewood, not briarwood," he yelped,
plucking the sharp thorns from his paws.

Later, when the pot was filled with water, the
Scruffy Varmint lay against a rock, licking his paws
and barking orders.

"Hustle, Bunnyrabbit. Get the flour."

"Yessir!" said Buddy.

"Five pinches of salt."
"Yessir!" said Buddy.
"Fifteen tomatoes."
"Yessir!" said Buddy.

"And a big load of squash."

"Yessir!" said Buddy.

The Scruffy Varmint rose and gave the soup a stir.

He took a taste. It tasted a little like . . . well,
a little . . . maybe it needed some pepper.

"Bunnyrabbit, get the pepper from the left side of the
kitchen sink," the Varmint growled.
"Who get the what from the where side of the where
what?" asked Buddy.

The Scruffy Varmint repeated, "WHO GET THE WHAT FROM THE WHERE SIDE OF THE WHERE WHAT? Never mind." He stalked into the kitchen and got the pepper himself and sprinkled it into the soup.

"There," he snarled. "Now, Bunnyrabbit, put the soup on the fire."

Buddy put the soup *in* the fire.

The fire went *Hssssssssss.*
So did the Scruffy Varmint.
"I'll teach you," he howled. "I WILL have soup!
Bunnyrabbit soup! And I know just the bunny to use,
the Bunnyrabbit who never listens!"
Buddy listened.

He also hopped.
Veryveryvery fast.
Faster than he had ever hopped in his life.

He whizzed up the road past the vegetable stand and into the safety of his house.

And a little later, when Buddy's parents
asked him to bring a pen and a slice of
bread, Buddy listened.

Me First

To my husband, Robin.

—H.L.

Pinkerton was pink, plump, and pushy.
He would do anything to be first, even if it meant
bouncing off bellies, stepping on snouts, or tying tails.

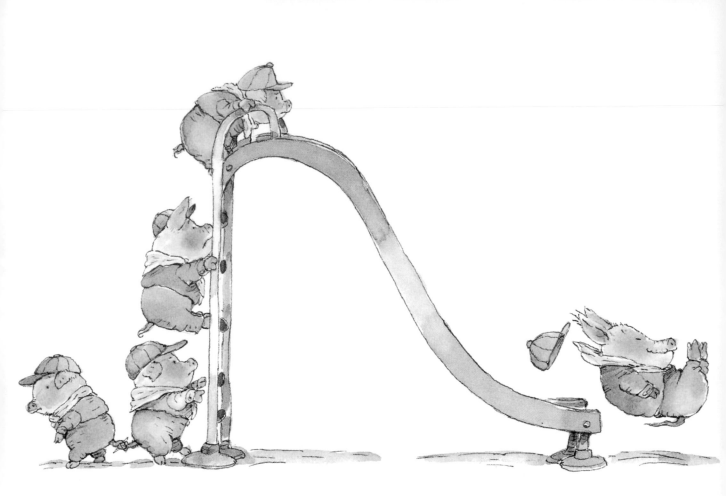

"Me first!" he cried when he had been last in line and finished first down the slide.

"Me first!" he cried at story time, settling on his round bottom with his big head right smack in front of the book.

And every day in the school trough-a-teria "Me first!"
rang out and there was Pinkerton.

One Saturday, Pinkerton's Pig Scout troop went on a day trip to the beach. Pinkerton was first on the bus and sat in the front row.

He was first off the bus,

first in the water,

first out of the water, and first into the picnic basket.

After lunch the Pig Scouts decided to go for a hike.
Off they went, with Pinkerton leading the line, of
course. As the Pig Scouts marched across the sand,
they heard a faint voice far in the distance.

The voice called out, "Who would care for a sandwich?"
Pinkerton pricked up his pointy ears.
Care for a sandwich?
Oh yes, me first! he thought,
and he began to trot ahead of the others.

Soon he heard the voice again, closer and louder this time.
"WHO WOULD CARE FOR A SANDWICH?"
"ME FIRST!" cried Pinkerton, kicking up sand and
leaving the other Pig Scouts far behind. His imagination
almost burst. Peanut butter! Jelly! Two tomatoes!
Seven pickles! A slab of cheese! A blob of mayo!
A big smear of mustard. All for ME! FIRST!

"WHO WOULD CARE FOR A SANDWICH?"

Now at a full gallop Pinkerton shrieked,
"ME FIRST!"
Over a sandy hill he flew and . . .
Kerplop.
He landed face to face with a small creature
with a bump on her nose and fur on her toes.

"Am I glad to see you!" she cackled.
"I sure could hear you coming:
'Me first. ME FIRST! ME FIRST!'
I guess you *really would* care for a sandwich."

"Oh, yes indeed," replied Pinkerton.
He jumped up and down so fast his teeth jiggled.

"Good!" cackled the small creature.

Pinkerton waited.
One second.
Two seconds.
Three seconds.
"Well?" he asked.
"Well what?" replied the small creature.
"The sandwich," begged Pinkerton.
"Where's . . . the sandwich?"

The small creature curtsied.
"You're looking at her."
She went on,
"I am a Sandwitch,
and I live in the sand,
and you said you would care for a Sandwitch,
so here I am. Care for me."

All Pinkerton could say was "But I . . ."
Taking no notice, the Sandwitch continued,
"You said, 'Me first.'
You wanted to be the first to care for me.
Well, congratulations!
Now just come along to my sand castle."
Grabbing Pinkerton firmly by the sleeve,
she led him around a few bends.

Before he could say "But I . . ." again, the gate to her
castle closed.

"All right, my pink, plump, and pushy one,
now you care for me. You may have the honor of being
the FIRST to powder my nose and comb my toes."

Seeing no way out, Pinkerton powdered her nose and combed her toes.

"Next," she crowed, "you may be the FIRST to put my supper in a bucket and feed me with a shovel."
Pinkerton looked around. He had no choice.
He put her supper in a bucket and fed her with a shovel.

Rubbing her tummy, the Sandwitch spoke on:
"Finally, after you've had the privilege of being the
FIRST to wash my dishes
    and sweep my castle
    and do my laundry
    and curl my hair
    and tuck me in,
you may be the FIRST to tell me a bedtime story."

Pinkerton washed the dishes,

swept the castle,

did the laundry,

curled the Sandwitch's hair, and tucked her in.

The Sandwitch stretched and yawned loudly.

"Now the story.

I need my story."

Pinkerton was so tired he could barely speak.

"I don't know any stories," he whimpered.

"Then how about making up something — oh, how about something concerning a pushy pig who always wanted to be first?"

Pinkerton sighed and began, "Once upon a time there lived a pig who always wanted to be first, until one day he met a wise Sandwitch —"

"Wise and beautiful," cut in the Sandwitch.

"— a wise and beautiful Sandwitch who showed him that FIRST was not always BEST."

"Aha!" cackled the Sandwitch.

She gave Pinkerton a slow, serious, and meaningful wink.

"Have you learned something?"

"Oh yes, yes, yes," said Pinkerton. "I promise I have."

"In that case, thanks for the care. Goodbye and good luck."

She opened the gate and Pinkerton sped off so fast he didn't even notice the delicious sandwich she held out to him.

He was just in time to catch the bus.
On he scooted — pink, plump, and glad to be last.

A Porcupine Named
Fluffy

When Mr. and Mrs. Porcupine had their first child, they were delighted. Now he needed a name.

Should they call him Spike?
No. Spike was too common.

Should they call him Lance?

No. Lance sounded too fierce.

Should they call him Needleroozer?

No. Needleroozer was too long.

Prickles? Pokey? Quillian?

Then together they had an idea.

"Let's call him Fluffy.

It's such a pretty name.

Fluffy!"

But soon there came a time when Fluffy
began to doubt that he was fluffy.

He first became suspicious when he backed into
a door and stuck fast.
That was not a fluffy thing to do.

He was even more convinced when he accidentally
slept on his back and poked holes in the mattress.
A very unfluffy thing to do.

When he tried to carry an umbrella he
knew the truth without a doubt.

Fluffy definitely wasn't.

So he decided to become fluffier.

"Clouds are fluffy," he thought. "I'll be a cloud."

But he couldn't stay up.

"I know. Pillows are fluffy!" he said. "I'll be a pillow."
But when his mother sat on him,
she was not pleased.

He tried soaking in a bubble bath for
forty-five minutes, but he did not become fluffy.
He became soggy.

He tried whipped cream.
He put a little on each quill. It was not easy,
and it took more than half a day.

But this did not make Fluffy fluffy.
"They should have named me Gooey," he sighed.

He ate a lot of fluffy marshmallows.

He rolled in shaving cream
and feathers.

He even tried to become a bunny.

But the truth remained.
Fluffy wasn't.

One afternoon Fluffy set out for a walk,
trying to think of ways to become fluffy.

Before long he met a very large rhinoceros.

"Grrrr!" said the rhinoceros. "I'm going
to give you a rough time."
Fluffy didn't know what a rough time was,
but he didn't like the sound of it at all.
"What is your name, small prickly thing?"
asked the rhinoceros unkindly.
"Fluffy," said Fluffy.

The rhinoceros smiled.
He giggled.
Then he laughed out loud.
He rolled on the ground.
He jiggled and slapped his knees.
He roared with laughter.

"A porcupine named Fluffy!" howled the rhinoceros.

Fluffy was embarrassed, but he tried to be polite.
"And what is *your* name?" he inquired.

"H . . . I can't say it," giggled the rhinoceros.

"Hubert?" suggested Fluffy.

"H . . . H . . . H . . . oh help, I just can't say it, I'm laughing so hard," said the rhinoceros.

"Harold? Or maybe Herman?" asked Fluffy.

"No," gasped the rhinoceros. "It's H . . . H . . . H . . . H . . . H . . .

. . . HIPPO."

Hippo.

A rhinoceros named Hippo.

Fluffy smiled.

He giggled.

Then he laughed out loud.

He jiggled and slapped his knees.

He howled with laughter.

"A rhinoceros named Hippo!" Fluffy cried.

A porcupine named Fluffy.
A rhinoceros named Hippo.
It was almost more than they could bear.
Hippo and Fluffy rolled on the ground giggling and laughing
until tears came to their eyes.

At last they lay exhausted on the ground.
From that time on they were the best of friends.

And Fluffy didn't mind being Fluffy anymore —
even though he wasn't.

Princess Penelope's Parrot

For *Allison Abbott,* a great educator and friend —H.L.

For *Linda* —L.M.

Princess Penelope's birthday was always a big occasion,
and this year was no exception.

Princess Penelope's dress had ruffles on its ruffles
on its ruffles.

Her presents were fabulous.
Roller blades studded with jewels.

A bathing suit woven from
rare peacock feathers.

A sixteen-wheeler.

The cake was seven layers high and
made with genuine llama's butter.
The top of the cake was decorated with
a golden cage. Within that golden cage
was a beautiful parrot.
"GIMME," said Princess Penelope,
her mouth stuffed with cake.
"GIMME, GIMME, GIMME."

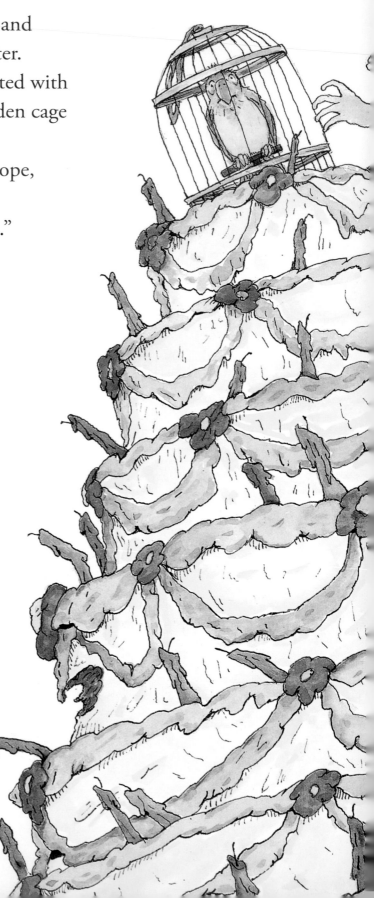

Quickly her servants stood one
on top of the other, plucked
the golden cage from the top
of the cake, and presented it.

167

"MINE," said the princess. "MINE, MINE, MINE."
Dribbling cake crumbs, she zoomed off to her chamber
with the cage.
Then she waited for the parrot to say something.
The parrot said nothing.

"TALK, BIG BEAK," demanded Princess Penelope.
The parrot said nothing.

"SPEAK, OR I'LL RATTLE YOUR CAGE."

The parrot said nothing, and Princess Penelope grew annoyed.

"ALL RIGHTY THEN, I'LL PUT YOU ON A BALL AND CHAIN."

The parrot looked miserable but said nothing.

Gritting her teeth, the princess hissed,
"LOOK, BIRDBRAIN, I'M ABOUT READY TO PLUCK YOUR
FEATHERS OUT ONE BY ONE."

Still the parrot said nothing.
Furious, Princess Penelope marched right up to the cage,
stared at the parrot nose to beak, and yelled,
"WHY DON'T YOU JUST GET LOST, KNOTHEAD?"

But the parrot did not get lost.
It stood in silence, nibbling forlornly
on the precious few birdseeds
the princess flicked its way.
Princess Penclope glared at the parrot,
snarling, "STUPID BUZZARD."

One day Princess Penelope received
a message that young Prince Percival
would be stopping by her palace on his
way to build sandcastles at the beach.

Although they had never met before, Princess Penelope
had long ago decided that she would marry Prince Percival
when she grew up. He was the richest prince
in the land. Not just a little rich.
But Rich, RICH, **RICH.**
She could just picture herself as Mrs. Prince Percival.
She'd have diamonds sparkling from every toe and finger
and a crown so heavy it would fold her ears.

The most precious of silks would cloak her right up to her royal nose.

Maybe her royal nose would have a golden nose ring.

She would make hundreds of lists for her servants.

Then she'd settle back on her velvet pillows to eat caviar cones and watch a twenty-foot TV all day long.

But enough dreaming.
Now she must get ready
to make a fine impression
on the prince.

She chose her poofiest dress,
arranged a new hairstyle,
and struggled into her highest heels.

As she clippy-clopped about, tidying her room (leaving out
only her most expensive toys), she came across the parrot.
Stupid buzzard, she thought.
Would the prince be impressed by this useless bird?
Absolutely not. Never.

So she hid the parrot behind the curtains.

There.

Now everything was perfect.

Princess Penelope put on her sweetest smile, sat upon her throne, and waited to dazzle the prince.

KaLUMP. KaLUMP. KaLUMP.

Princess Penelope put her hand to her ear.

This must be her prince!

KaLUMP. KaLUMP. KaLUMP.

She could just imagine him galloping up on his fine white horse.

KaLUMP. KaLUMP. KaLUMP.
Prince Percival galloped into Princess Penelope's chamber.
No horse. But impressive feet. And nice shoes.
Whoosh. Prince Percival bowed deeply and held out a
huge bouquet of roses.

"GIMME," said the parrot from behind the curtain.
"GIMME, GIMME, GIMME."
Prince Percival gulped and handed over the roses.

"MINE," squawked the parrot.

"MINE, MINE, MINE."

Prince Percival's eyebrows twitched. How could someone with such a sweet smile say such rude things?

"TALK, BIG BEAK."

The prince scratched his nose and thought that just maybe he wanted to be somewhere else.

Then the parrot screamed,
"SPEAK OR I'LL RATTLE YOUR CAGE."
Cage? Cage? Prince Percival
felt trapped. As he moved toward
the door the parrot screeched on,
"ALL RIGHTY THEN, I'LL PUT YOU ON
A BALL AND CHAIN.
LOOK, BIRDBRAIN, I'M ABOUT
READY TO PLUCK YOUR
FEATHERS OUT ONE BY ONE."
That did it. Prince Percival bolted
out the door and galloped off.
KaLUMP. KaLUMP. KaLUMP.

Princess Penelope followed. Clippy-Cloppy.
Clippy-Cloppy. Clippy-Cloppy.
And the parrot flapped after them both, ball,
chain, and all. Up and down staircases, past
the birthday present room, and through the kitchen they
KaLUMPED and Clippy-Clopped and flapped.
As Prince Percival finally galloped out the
palace door into the safety of the green
fields the parrot called out,
"WHY DON'T YOU JUST GET LOST, KNOTHEAD?"
Prince Percival was delighted to do so and
didn't stop once until he'd made it all the
way to the beach.

In the palace doorway the parrot cocked its head at
Princess Penelope and cheerfully said, "STUPID BUZZARD."
Then it stepped out of the ball and chain and flew away.
The prince and the parrot lived together happily ever after.

Princess Penelope was horribly embarrassed.
But she got over it.
And in no time she went right to work in front of
her mirror, practicing her sweetest smile —
just in case the second richest prince in the land
should come her way one day.

The Wizard, the Fairy, and the Magic Chicken

There once lived a Wizard, a Fairy, and a Magic Chicken.
Each thought, "I am the greatest in the world."
And each was very jealous of the other two.

"MY wand has a MOON on it," said the Wizard.

"MY wand has a STAR on it," said the Fairy.
"MY wand has a PICKLE on it,"
said the Magic Chicken.

"I can kiss a pig

and turn it into a bicycle," said the Wizard.

"That's nothing," said the Fairy. "*I* can kiss a bicycle
and turn it into a bowl of soup."

"I can do better than that,"
said the Magic Chicken.
"*I* can kiss a bowl of soup
and turn it into a singing frog."

Each one always tried to outdo the others.

"I can make a hairy
monster with sharp teeth!"
bellowed the Wizard.

"*I* can make a bumpy monster with nine legs!"
screeched the Fairy.

"*I* can make a dotted monster with buggy eyes!"
yelled the Magic Chicken.

The monsters glared at the magicians and loudly said,

"GRRRRRROLPH!"

For the very first time the magicians agreed.

"RUN FOR YOUR LIVES!" they shouted.

"I will make a cloud to hide behind," gasped the Wizard,
but that didn't stop the monsters.

"I will make thunder to scare them," puffed the Fairy,
but the monsters were not frightened.

"I will make lightning. That will make them go away,"
cried the Magic Chicken, but they would not go away.
Nothing worked.

"We'd better . . ." said the Wizard.

". . . try something . . ." said the Fairy.

". . . together!" said the Magic Chicken.

So they chanted, "One, two, three, *GO!*"
The cloud and the thunder and the lightning came together.
Suddenly it rained.

It rained so hard and the monsters got so wet that they shrank
until they were only very little monsters and
not scary at all.

"We did it!" cheered the Wizard, the Fairy, and the Magic Chicken.

"I must say, though," said the Wizard, "my cloud made the rain."

"Well," said the Fairy, "it was because of my thunder."

"But not without my lightning," said the Magic Chicken.

There once lived a Wizard, a Fairy, and a Magic Chicken.
They argued a lot, but deep down they were very good
friends.

The Sheep in Wolf's Clothing

To my son Jamie, with thanks for thinking of . . . *Mother.*
—H.L.

Ewetopia was not comfortable in her own wool.
She always needed to hide in an outfit, and spent a fortune
on her clothes.
But no one paid any attention.

She attempted to dazzle the rams.

But Rambunctious, Ramshackle, and Ramplestiltskin barely blinked.

She even tried to shock the other ewes.

But Ewecalyptus, Ewetensil, and Heyewe hardly noticed.

This lack of attention annoyed Ewetopia like a bad itch.

Then one fine day she received an invitation to the Woolyones'
Costume Ball.

Yes! Here was her chance.

She'd have the finest costume in Pastureland and outshine them
all. Every fluffy one. Ha!

In a frenzy of excitement, Ewetopia tried
on fifty-seven costumes. Her clothes-changing
muscles were aching—almost worn out—
when she put on outfit number fifty-eight.

That settled it. This was the one! Ewereka!

She loved the warmth of the fur. The shine of the fangs. And especially
the way the long-clawed paws swung attractively when she walked.
Everyone would notice her now!

On the eve of the Woolyones' Costume Ball, Ewetopia arrived with her heart aflutter.

She waited for someone to invite her to dance.

And waited. And waited.

And while she waited, the ewes and rams did sheeptrots and waltzes, and gathered in small groups to whisper and point.

"Shhhhh. Bad taste," remarked Ewecalyptus and Ewetensil.

"Shhhhh. Faulty judgment," added Heyewe.

"Shhhhh. One wonders what sort of family she comes from," wondered Rambunctious and Ramshackle.

"Shhhhh. Cotton-brained idea!" pronounced Ramplestiltskin.

Then all of a sudden as the sheep waltzed and whispered and
Ewetopia waited, a stranger entered the ballroom. A handsome
stranger, a charming sheepish grin, and wool so lovely,
it looked fake.
The sheep were so taken with the beauty of this creature, none
stopped to wonder why a sheep would go to a costume ball dressed
as a . . . *sheep*.
The flock gawked.

Ewetopia approached the stranger.
The stranger approached Ewetopia.
From under his sheep costume the newcomer could
see the fur, the fangs, and the long, sharp claws.
It had to be.

In a low, growly voice he exclaimed, "MOTHER!"
Mother? Beneath her costume, Ewetopia blinked.
Mother? She knitted her eyebrows (a sheep thing).
"Mother," growled the creature, "I thought you were
away on a lamb hunt."
Lamb hunt?

Ewetopia found this puzzling, but she did
need a partner, and so their dance began.

"Ah, Mother, Mother," the stranger growled in one ear.
"I've missed your home cooking," he growled in the other ear.
"Especially the ewe stew with ram ramen."

Then he growled in both ears,
"Let us grab a couple of fat woolyones, leave this silly ball,
go home, and dine on sheep."

Ewetopia sensed that something was wrong.
Dine on sheep? What kind of a creep would dine on a sheep?

For the first time Ewetopia noticed her ex-partner's long, sharp claws and extremely hairy feet.

And then it hit her.

She had not been dancing with a sheep dressed as a sheep at all.

Oh, no. She had been dancing with a real *wolf*. Big, bad, and mistaking her for his mother!

This varmint posed a danger not only to her but to all those in the ballroom.

Indeed he did, for just then he ripped off his
costume and growled, "Come on, Mother. Let's eat!"
With that he snatched Ewecalyptus, Ewetensil, and Heyewe
and stuffed them into a sack.

The woolyones gasped in
horror and ran for their lives.

What to do?

No time for wooly-brained thoughts.
Ewetopia paced in circles.
Mother . . . mother . . . mother . . .
He thinks I'm his mother!

Then she stood up as straight as she could in her foolish
costume, lowered her voice to a growl, and announced,
"Sonny dearest, I have a surprise for you."

"Surprise!" growled the wolf. He loved surprises and would have squealed with delight, but wolves aren't good at squealing. Ewetopia needed to stall for time, as she hadn't the foggiest idea what the surprise might be. So she tried to think of motherly things to say.

"First, my son, before the surprise you must take a *bath*,
clean your *claws,* and brush your *fangs.*"

The wolf moaned, "Aw, Maaaaaaa."

"After that you must do your homework. All of it."

The wolf whined, "Mommmmmmeeeeee."

"Then, sonny boy, you *must* pick up your room."
That did it.

He threw himself onto the floor and into a full-blown, out-of-control tantrum.

"I WON'T! I WON'T!"
He kicked his feet.

"YOU CAN'T MAKE ME!"
He pounded his furry fists.

"I DON'T HAVE TO,
SO THERE SO THERE
SO THERE!"

So great was his tantrum
that within less than a
minute he was completely
exhausted and unable to move.

It was then that Ewetopia knew
what the surprise would be.

She flipped off her furry costume, bent over the helpless wolf, and announced, "Surprise! I'm a ewe!"

The wolf opened one eye. "You're not a me. I'm a me. You're a you."

"That's what I said." Ewetopia smiled. "I'm a ewe."

"Who's a who?" The wolf was flustered.

And Ewetopia repeated, "I'm a ewe."

This was too much for the wolf's small brain to process. Muttering "I'm not a you. You're a you. I'm a me. I came in as a me, and I'll leave as a me," he dragged his weary self to the door, forgetting all about dinner.

He paused and gave one last howl:
"And I'll never ever EVER pick up my room!"

With a stomp and a thomp, he was gone. Ewecalyptus, Ewetensil, and Heyewe scrambled out of the sack and hugged Ewetopia.

Everyone in the ballroom sang out,
"What kind of a creep would dine on a sheep?"

For the rest of the evening Ewetopia had a ball.

She danced with Ewecalyptus, and Rambunctious, and Ewetensil, and Ramshackle, and Heyewe, and Ramplestiltskin.
And she felt entirely comfortable in her own wool.

Meet the Author and Illustrator

Helen Lester and Lynn Munsinger have been together through thick and thin since first publishing *The Wizard, the Fairy, and the Magic Chicken* in 1983. They have collaborated on the hilarious Tacky the Penguin series and many other wildly funny and popular titles, including the award-winning *Hooway for Wodney Wat*. Helen Lester is a full-time writer who makes her home in New York, and Lynn Munsinger is a full-time illustrator living in Vermont. Visit www.helenlester.com to learn more about their many books.

LOOK FOR ALL OF THE LAUGH-ALONG LESSONS!

To see book descriptions and download discussion and activity guides, visit www.hmhbooks.com/laughalonglessons.